Little Red Hen's Great Escape

by Elizabeth Dale

and Andrew Painter

This story is based on the traditional fairy tale, *The Little Red Hen*, but with a new twist. You can read the original story in Must Know Stories. Can you make up your own twist for the story?

Franklin Watts
First published in Great Britain in 2015 by The Watts Publishing Group

ISBN 978 1 4451 4304 0 (hbk)
ISBN 978 1 4451 4305 7 (pbk)
ISBN 978 1 4451 4307 1 (library ebook)

Series Editor: Melanie Palmer
Series Advisor: Catherine Glavina
Series Designer: Peter Scoulding
Cover Designer: Cathryn Gilbert

Printed in China

Franklin Watts
An imprint of
Hachette Children's Group
Part of The Watts Publishing Group
Carmelite House
50 Victoria Embankment
London EC4Y 0DZ

An Hachette UK Company
www.hachette.co.uk

www.franklinwatts.co.uk

MIX
Paper from responsible sources
FSC® C104740

The Little Red Hen was worried. Bulldozers had arrived in the farmyard. Holes were being dug. Something bad was going on.

She went to see Farmer Green. She knew he wouldn't tell her what was happening, so she had to be clever.

"The builders are so busy,"
she clucked. "Can I help?"

"You!" laughed the farmer.
"How can you help?"

"I can pick up sand and straw to keep everywhere tidy," the Little Red Hen said.

“OK,” said the farmer.
“Be helpful while you can.”
The Little Red Hen trembled
with fear. What did he mean?

“Something terrible is happening,” she told the pig, the lamb and the duck. “Please help me to find out what it is!”

"Not until eleven o'cluck!"

snorted the pig.

"No thank ewe,"

laughed the lamb.

"You're just chicken!" quacked the duck.

"Lazy animals!" thought the Little Red Hen.

“Something terrible’s happening,” she told the chickens. “Please help me find out what.”

"What are you, the little Head Hen?" clucked one.

"No," said the Little Red Hen. "But we're in danger. No one else will help."

The poor Little Red Hen looked so worried.

"OK!" said the chickens.

"Brilliant!" clucked the Little Red Hen. "Keep your beaks to the ground, your eyes wide open and report back."

So the chickens scurried all over the farmyard, beaks to the ground, eyes wide open. So did the chicks.

Some chickens picked up sand, while some pecked through a big cloth. Others flew around the farm, while the Little Red Hen read the plans.

They all met back in the barn.

"There are piles of bricks!" clucked one chick.

"Steel doors!" said another.

"Big walls!" said a third.

“They’re planning to keep every animal cooped up inside!” cried the Little Red Hen. “We must tell the others!”

“You need some oinkment!” snorted the pig.

“You’re utterly quackers!” quacked the duck.

"You're baaa–king maaaad!" bleated the lamb.

"Well, all the chickens are leaving!" said the Little Red Hen.

And they did.

The next day, the farmer came
to fetch all the animals.
"Come for a lovely walk,"
he told them.

“Isn’t he nice,” said the pig, the lamb and the duck. “The Little Red Hen was just being silly!”

"In you come," smiled the farmer, opening up a door.

"Help!" cried the pig, the lamb and the duck.

The chickens pushed the farmer inside! Clunk! went the door. Click! went the key.

"Hooray!" cried the pig, the lamb
and the duck, making faces
at the farmer.

To celebrate their escape, the animals had a brilliant party.

“Please help clean up!” said the Little Red Hen. So the animals did – after all, they’d learned their lesson.

Puzzle 1

Put these pictures in the correct order.
Which event do you think is most important?
Now try writing the story in your own words!

Puzzle 2

1. I have got a surprise for the animals!

2. I have found a secret plan.

3. We work well as a team.

4. There is lots of work to do.

5. We have been spying.

6. Something isn't right on the farm.

Choose the correct speech bubbles for each character. Can you think of any others? Turn over to find the answers.

Answers

Puzzle 1

The correct order is: 1c, 2f, 3e, 4a, 5b, 6d

Puzzle 2

The Little Red Hen: 2, 6

The farmer: 1, 4

The chicks: 3, 5